Bodhidharma Cave
Shaolin Temple
Dengfeng
River
River
River

Ming's Kung Fu Adventure

in the Shaolin Temple

This book is edited and designed by the Editorial Committee of *Cultural China* series

Story and Illustrations: Li Jian
Translation: Yijin Wert

Editorial Assistant: Zhang Mengke
Editors: Yang Xiaohe, Anna Nguyen
Editorial Director: Zhang Yicong

Senior Consultants: Sun Yong, Wu Ying, Yang Xinci
Managing Director and Publisher: Wang Youbu

ISBN: 978-1-60220-992-3

Address any comments about *Ming's Kung Fu Adventure in the Shaolin Temple: A Zen Buddhist Tale in English and Chinese* to:

Better Link Press
99 Park Ave
New York, NY 10016
USA

or

Shanghai Press and Publishing Development Company
F 7 Donghu Road, Shanghai, China (200031)
Email: comments_betterlinkpress@hotmail.com

Printed in China by Shenzhen Donnelley Printing Co., Ltd.

1 3 5 7 9 10 8 6 4 2

少林寺

Ming's Kung Fu Adventure in the Shaolin Temple

A Zen Buddhist Tale in English and Chinese

by Li Jian
Translated by Yijin Wert

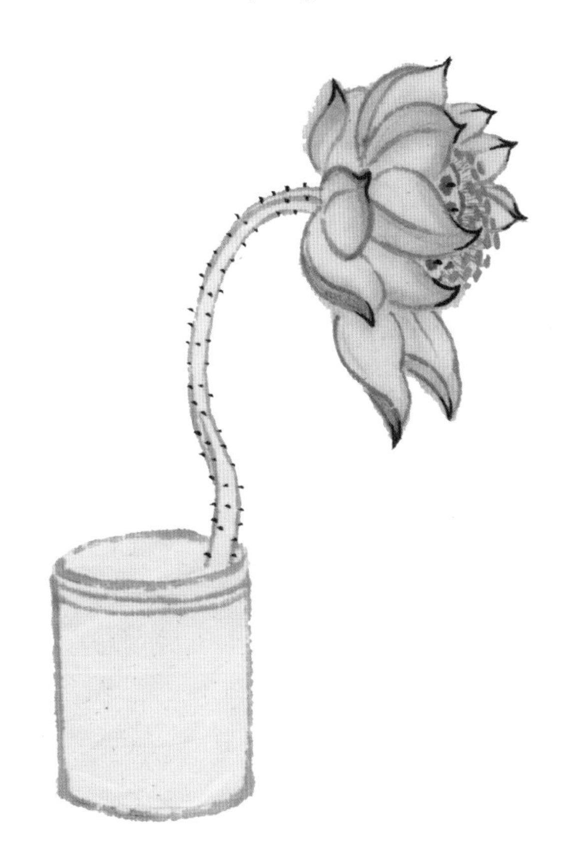

Better Link Press

嵩山少林

Ming could hardly contain his excitement when he found out his school would offer Kung Fu classes. To show Ming its rich history, his parents took him to visit the Shaolin Temple of Henan Province in China, the birth place of Kung Fu.

得知学校要开功夫课，小明兴奋极了。为了让小明了解它深厚的历史文化，爸爸妈妈带他到功夫的诞生地——中国河南登封的少林寺旅行。

When Ming and his parents entered into the courtyard outside the Shaolin Temple, they saw some young men practicing Kung Fu.

当小明一家来到少林寺外的广场时，看见一些年青人在练武。

Drawn by their graceful and clean movements, Ming tried his best to copy the young men. A boy in the group noticed Ming, and came over to help him by correcting his movements. They quickly became good friends.

小明被他们飘逸又整齐的动作吸引住了，就尝试跟着学了起来。队伍中的一个男孩留意到了小明，跑过来帮他纠正姿势。他们很快就成了朋友。

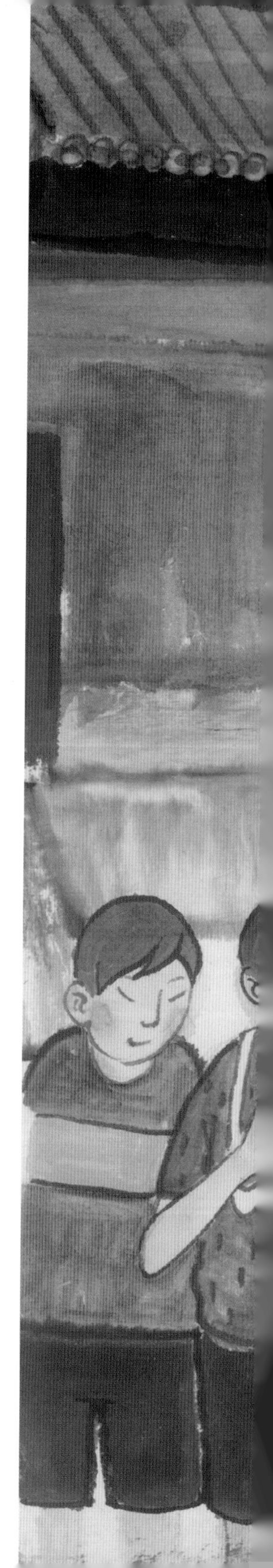

The boy's name was Joe. "I know a master whose Kung Fu skills are much better, but we may have to look in several places to find him," he said.

男孩叫乔。他说："我知道有一位师父的功夫更棒，不过我们得跑几个地方找找他。"

禪

They came to the gate of the temple where Joe used to see the master, but he wasn't there.

他们来到少林寺的山门，乔在这里见过那位师父。不过，他不在这里。

少林寺

Then they checked at the Mahavira Hall where Joe used to see the master, but he wasn't there.

他们随后去大雄宝殿看了看，乔在这里见过那位师父。不过，他不在这里。

大雄寶殿

They walked next to the Thousand-Buddha Hall and had to continue along to another area.

他们之后走到了千佛殿，不过还得接着去别的地方找。

They stopped at the Pagoda Forest where Joe used to see the master, but he wasn't there.

他们去了塔林，乔在这里见过那位师父。不过，他不在这里。

Lastly, Joe thought the master could be in the mountains behind the temple. Joe led Ming to some stone stairs, which began their difficult ascent.

最后，乔想到师父可能在寺后的山中。他带着小明登上石阶，开始艰难的攀登。

On the mountain, they stopped in front of a cave, but nobody was there. Ming felt discouraged after what seemed like an endless search. He thought that they would never find the master.

他们在山上的一个石洞前停了下来，但里面没人。寻找似乎没有尽头，小明有些气馁。他想大概找不到那位师父了。

Suddenly, someone came out of the cave and greeted them, "Hello!"

"Master, my friend Ming comes with me to learn Kung Fu with you." Joe answered happily in surprise.

The master said, "Welcome!"

这时，有人进洞来问候他们说：“你们好！”

乔又惊讶又高兴：“师父，我带了新朋友小明来跟你学功夫。”

师父说：“好呀！”

The master practiced a set of Kung Fu movements gracefully and smoothly. Joe told Ming quietly that this was the Shaolin Luohan Quan, the most well-known type of Shaolin Kung Fu.

师父打了一套拳，他的动作如行云流水。乔悄声告诉小明，那是少林寺最著名的功夫罗汉拳。

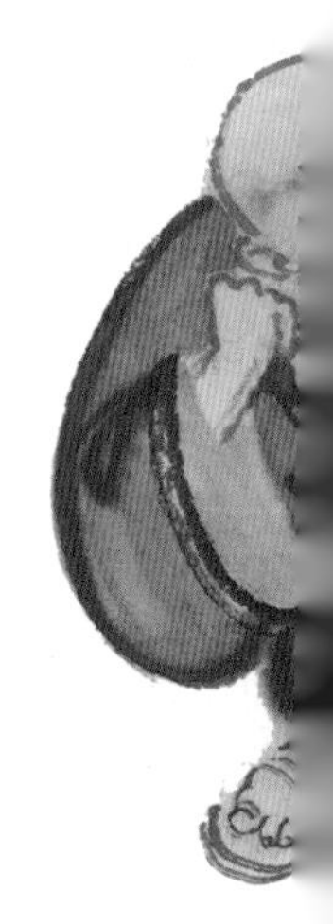

The master then sat down and said, “Do you know that the Shaolin Temple is famous not only for Kung Fu, but also for Zen? Let me tell you a story about it.”

师父随后坐下说：“你们知道么？少林寺最出名的除了功夫，还有禅。我来给你们讲一个禅的故事吧。”

Hello~
Hello~

While a little boy was climbing the mountains, he shouted "Hello" to the mountains.

Suddenly, the sound echoed everywhere around him in the mountains.

一个孩子在爬山的时候，无意间对着大山喊了一声"喂……"

声音刚落，从四面八方传来了阵阵"喂……"的回声。

In shock, the boy shouted out, “Who are you?”

Then the mountains answered, “Who are you?”

The boy cried out, “Why don’t you tell me first?”

The mountains simply replied, “Why don’t you tell me first? Why don’t you tell me first?”

孩子很惊讶，喊道：“你是谁？”

然后大山回应道：“你是谁？”

孩子大喊：“为什么你不先说？”

大山又大声回应说：“为什么你不先说？为什么你不先说？”

Who are you?
Who are you?

I hate you!

The boy got very angry and shouted, "I hate you!"
Then he heard the mountains saying, "I hate you! I hate you!"

孩子生气了，喊道："我恨你！"
随后，他听到大山说："我恨你！我恨你！"

The boy ran back home with tears in his eyes. He told his mother about what happened in the mountains. His mother said to him, "Why don't you go back there and shout 'I love you'? Then you can see what will happen."

孩子哭着跑回家，告诉妈妈山里发生的事。妈妈对孩子说："你回去对着大山喊'我爱你'，试试看会怎样，好吗？"

I love you!
I love you!

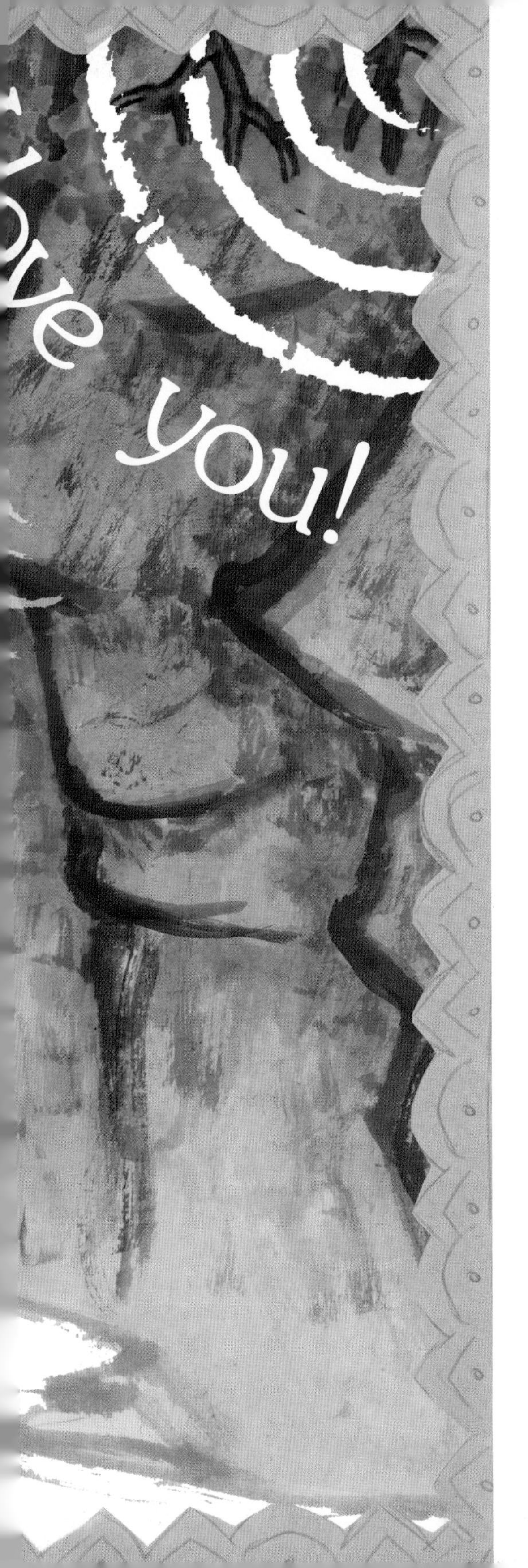

The boy ran back to the mountains to shout out "I love you!"

He was then surrounded by the echoing sound "I love you". The boy laughed.

The master said: "So gaining happiness is the wisdom of Zen."

孩子又跑回山里，大喊“我爱你！”

随后他被包围在“我爱你”的回声中，孩子笑了。

师父说：“所以，获得快乐就是禅的智慧。”

While Ming and Joe listened intently to the story, Ming heard his father calling him from outside the cave. The master had disappeared when they came back inside.

当小明和乔正听得入神时，洞外传来爸爸寻找小明的喊声。他们再回洞里时，那位师父已经不见了。

Cultural Explanation
知识点

Zen Buddhism, Kung Fu and Shaolin Temple
禅宗、功夫和少林寺

The Shaolin Temple, located in Henan Province, 13 kilometers to the northwest of Dengfeng City, was built in 495. An Indian master called Bodhidharma (?–536) came to the temple in 527 to spread Zen Buddhism teachings and became known as the founder of Chinese Zen Buddhism. The Shaolin Temple is regarded as its birthplace.

Zen Buddhism teachings say that being quiet and eliminating distractions can produce physical and mental relaxation. It also gives Shaolin Kung Fu its profound cultural content, therefore the "unity of Zen and Martial arts" is the ideal state of Shaolin Kung Fu.

少林寺始建于公元495年，位于中国河南省登封市西北13公里。527年，印度高僧菩提达摩（? —536）来到少林寺传授禅宗，他因此成为中国佛教禅宗的创始人，少林寺遂成为禅宗祖庭。

禅宗主张安静、停止杂虑，久而久之可达身心轻松。禅宗赋予了少林功夫深厚的文化内涵，"禅武合一"是修习少林功夫的理想境界。

Memorial Archway

It is one or two kilometers away from the Mountain Gate.

牌坊

从牌坊开始，一两公里就到山门了。

Temple Gate

It consists of the main gate, western and eastern wicket gates.

山门

少林寺的山门由正门和东西掖门组成。

Mahavira Hall

Monks at Shaolin Temple chant sutras and deal with Buddhism affairs in this hall.

大雄宝殿

少林僧人在此诵经，并安排佛事活动。

Thousand-Buddha Hall

There is a fresco of five hundred arhats here. Monks used to practice martial arts here. There are holes in the ground from the monks practicing Kung Fu.

千佛殿

这里有五百罗汉壁画。地面的坑凹是僧人在此习武时留下的。

Pagoda Forest

It is the graveyard of monks with great achievement. With more than 230 ancient pagodas, it is the largest forest of pagodas in China.

塔林

有成就僧人的墓地。有230余座古塔，是中国规模最大的塔林。

Bodhidharma Cave

It is located on a mountain peak which is about two kilometers to the northwest of the temple. It is said to be the place where Bodhidharma faced the wall to meditate. A statue of Bodhidharma is inside.

达摩洞

位于少林寺西北约2公里的山峰上，传说为达摩面壁修行处，内供达摩塑像。

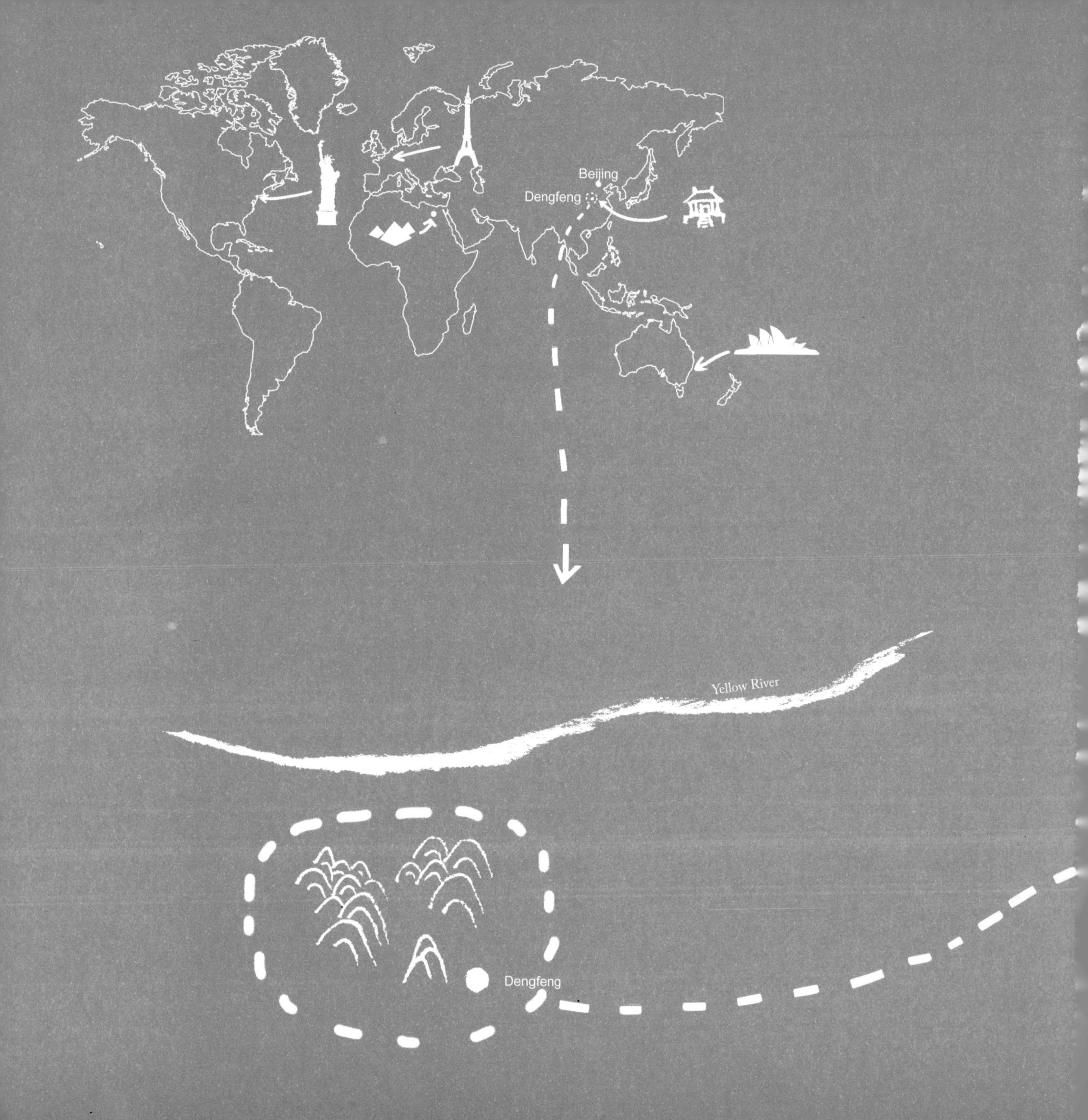
Beijing
Dengfeng
Yellow River
Dengfeng